FRIGHTVILLE

DON'T LET THE DOLL IN

FRIGHTVILLE

DON'T LET THE DOLL IN

BY MIKE FORD

Scholastic Inc.

Copyright © 2019 by Mike Ford
Photos ©: cover font and throughout: Doctor Letters/Shutterstock.

All rights reserved. Published by Scholastic Inc., *Publishers since 1920*. SCHOLASTIC and associated logos are trademarks and/or registered trademarks of Scholastic Inc.

The publisher does not have any control over and does not assume any responsibility for author or third-party websites or their content.

No part of this publication may be reproduced, stored in a retrieval system, or transmitted in any form or by any means, electronic, mechanical, photocopying, recording, or otherwise, without written permission of the publisher. For information regarding permission, write to Scholastic Inc., Attention: Permissions Department, 557 Broadway, New York, NY 10012.

ISBN 978-1-338-36009-7

10 9 8 7 6 5 4 3 2 1   19 20 21 22 23

Printed in the U.S.A.   40
First printing September 2019

Book design by Stephanie Yang

FOR ANNABELLE

1

"Mara! We're going to be late!"

Mara ignored her father's call. She was painting the window trim in the attic bedroom, and was nearly finished.

"Mara!" her father called again, a little more loudly.

"You'd better go," her mother said. "This can wait."

Mara set her paintbrush down and untied

the strings of the apron she had on over her school clothes. "All right," she said as she hung the apron on a hook. "But don't do any more work until I get home. Promise."

"I promise," her mother said. "I have to work on the plans for the Hudsons' house today anyway."

Mara went over to where her mother was seated at her drafting table and gave her a hug. "I'm sure the house you're designing for them is nice," she said. "But not as nice as *my* house."

Her mother laughed. "Of course not," she said. "I save all my best ideas for you."

"Mara!"

"Coming!" Mara shouted as she took one last look at the huge dollhouse sitting on the workbench and reluctantly went downstairs.

Her father was waiting by the front door, the car keys in his hand. Mara's little brother, Jesse, was standing beside him, his backpack on and an impatient look on his seven-year-old face.

"Sorry," Mara said as she grabbed her coat from the closet and snatched up her own backpack. "We were working on the house."

"We're going to be *late*," Jesse said. "And I have a spelling test today."

"Which I'm sure you'll get a perfect score on," Mara said, putting her arm around him as they exited the house. "I'll quiz you on the way to school."

As she predicted, he got every word right. Mara, however, realized that she'd left her math homework sitting on the desk in her room and her gym clothes on top of the dryer, where her father had left them for her.

It was going to be that kind of day.

"I'll see you this afternoon," her father called out the car window as Mara and Jesse walked into school. "Love you!"

"Love you back!" Mara and Jesse shouted in unison.

Once they were inside the doors of Crowleyville Central School, Jesse headed left to the second-grade classrooms while Mara turned right and went up the stairs to where the fifth-grade rooms were. When she got to homeroom, she found everyone standing around Krish Dhawan's desk. Mara hung up her coat and put her things away in her cubby, then went to see what all the excitement was about.

"What's going on?" she asked as she peered

over the shoulder of her best friend, Olivia Winters. Krish had what looked like several small action figures set out on his desk.

"I think this one is my favorite," Krish said, picking up one of the figures and holding it out for everyone to see. "He's called the Fishman of the Lost Lagoon."

Mara leaned over and picked up one of the other figures.

"That one is the Werewolf Bride," Krish told her. "Look at the flowers in her crown. They're covered in *blood*."

"She's cool," said Mara. "And the perfect size to live in my dollhouse."

"Maybe if your dollhouse was a castle in Transylvania," Olivia joked.

"Where'd you get these?" Mara asked Krish.

"This awesome new store," said Krish. "Frightville. It just opened. It's across the street from the grocery store, between Comicland and the Dirty Dog Wash-a-teria. They sell all kinds of weird stuff."

Before Mara could ask any more questions, Ms. Taggart came in. "All right, everyone," she said cheerfully. "I hope you're ready for a pop quiz on algae and fungi."

Mara handed the Werewolf Bride back to Krish and took her seat. Ms. Taggart passed out the quizzes, and soon the room was filled with the sound of scribbling pencils. Thankfully, reading chapter seven in her science textbook was the one thing Mara had remembered to do, and so she answered the questions quickly, although on the section where she had to label the parts of a mushroom, she had to guess on a couple.

The rest of the class was a lecture about spores. Mara tried to listen, but mostly she was thinking about her dollhouse. She and her mother had been working on it for months. They'd started over summer break, drawing up the plans and then cutting the pieces and nailing and gluing them together. Now it was October. Everything had taken a long time because Mara wanted it to be perfect. And it was. Almost.

The one thing she didn't have for the house was someone to live in it. She'd been so busy building it, she hadn't even thought about what kind of person might want to live in the house.

The house was a big Victorian-style three-story, with a tower and an attic bedroom and all kinds of neat things her mother had designed. Mara wished she could live in a house like that too. Not that there was anything wrong with her actual house, but it was a little ordinary compared to the dollhouse. And an interesting house needed someone interesting to live in it.

At lunchtime, Mara sat with Olivia and Krish and some of the other kids from her class. Mara used the opportunity to ask Krish more about the store where he'd gotten his monster action figures.

"Do they have, you know, anything a little less creepy?" she asked.

"What, you don't want vampires and zombies living in your dollhouse?" Max Gershwin joked. "I think a haunted dollhouse would be awesome."

"They have all kinds of stuff," Krish assured Mara. "You should just go check it out."

Mara decided she would.

———————————

When her father met her and Jesse outside school that afternoon, she asked if they could make a detour on the way home.

"Sure," her father said. "I need to pick up a few things at the grocery store for dinner anyway. I'll drop you and Jesse off at—what did you call it?"

"Frightville," Mara said.

"Frightville," her father said, chuckling. "Sounds like a convenience store for witches. Pick up some eye of newt for me, okay? I'll add it to the goulash I'm making for dinner."

"Will do, Dad," Mara said, looking at Jesse and rolling her eyes.

A few minutes later, they pulled into the parking lot of Frightville. Mara and Jesse got out of the car.

"The grocery store is right across the street," their father said, pointing to it as if they hadn't been inside it a bunch of times. "I'll be done in twenty minutes. Don't go anywhere else, okay?"

"Got it," Mara assured him. "Can we at least take candy from strangers if we run into any?"

"Only if it's chocolate," her father said, pretending to be serious. "None of those licorice drops or gummy pumpkins, though."

Mara laughed. "Okay, Dad," she said as Jesse pulled her toward the store. "See you in a little while."

2

Mara pushed open the door to the shop. A low, moaning wail filled the air.

"Welcome to Frightville," said a creaky voice.

At first Mara thought the greeting was part of the recording. Then a tall, thin man appeared from out of the shadows. He was wearing an old-fashioned black suit and a gray shirt with a black tie, and his silver hair was slicked back over his head. With his pale white skin, he looked like a character who had stepped out of a black-and-white movie.

"Allow me to introduce myself," he said. "I am Odson Ends, the proprietor of this establishment."

"I'm Mara," said Mara. "And this is Jesse."

"A pleasure to meet you both," said Mr. Ends, the corners of his mouth turning up in the barest hint of a smile. "May I ask what brings you into my little shop today?"

"My friend Krish was here yesterday," Mara answered. "He bought some awesome figurines."

Mr. Ends nodded. "I remember," he said. "From the Monstertown collection. Very popular. Are you looking to get some for yourself?

I believe I still have Count Fangtooth and Lady Wrappers, the singing mummy."

Mara shook her head. "They're not exactly what I'm looking for," she said.

"Mara doesn't play with monsters," Jesse announced. "She likes *dolls*."

"I built a dollhouse," Mara explained. "With my mother. Now I'm looking for someone to live in it. But I don't want any ordinary old doll. I want something special. Something nobody else has."

"I see," said Mr. Ends. "You're in search of a unique tenant." He tapped his chin and looked at Mara with eyes that she realized now were the color of thunderstorms. "I think I might have something you'll like."

Jesse wandered off to look at something

that had caught his attention, and Mara followed Mr. Ends as he walked through the store.

"Every item in my shop is unusual, of course," Mr. Ends said as they walked. "But some are more unusual than others. I keep my extra-special merchandise back here."

He stopped in front of an antique cabinet with glass doors. Behind the glass was an array of objects: carved wooden animals, old metal keys, a clock with the face of a clown, windup toys, what looked like a small brass telescope. Mr. Ends drew a skeleton key from his pocket and slipped it into a lock on the cabinet doors. He turned it. There was a click, and then the doors swung open.

"These objects are particularly unique," Mr. Ends said. "Some people even believe they have a bit of magic in them."

"Magic?" said Mara. She laughed. "Like they can grant wishes?"

Mr. Ends smiled. "Who's to say? Why don't you take a look and see if you find an inhabitant for your special house? There are several here that might be suitable. If you require any assistance, please ask."

He walked away, leaving Mara to examine the contents of the cabinet. Her eyes scanned the shelves, looking for dolls. She found one right away. It was a magician carved out of wood. His suit was black with gold buttons. He had a top hat on his head and a wand in his hand. He even had a painted-on mustache. He was neat, but he didn't look like he belonged in Mara's house. She set him back on the shelf.

She looked some more, passing up a ballerina, a butcher wearing a stained apron and holding a cleaver, and a pair of twin boy dolls wearing matching blue shorts, red-and-white-striped shirts, and sailor hats.

And then she saw it. Tucked into a corner, almost hidden behind a ceramic dragon, was another doll. It was a girl, about five inches high. Mara picked her up. Her body was made out of snow-white porcelain. She was wearing a dark red velvet dress, with tiny pearls sewn all around the collar. Her long black hair was tied back with a red ribbon, and when Mara ran her fingers over the hair, it felt real. Her face was painted on. She had brown eyes, pink cheeks, and a red mouth. Around her neck was a real gold chain with a tiny locket hanging from it. On her feet were tiny black slippers.

Mara examined the doll more closely, and saw that the dress had pockets. Something was sticking out of one of them. Mara picked at it and pulled out a small envelope. Inside was a tiny piece of paper. The writing was too small to read, and she could only make out the beginning.

"My dear Charlotte," Mara read. She looked at the doll. "Is that your name? Charlotte?"

She wondered who had made the doll. It looked quite old. Had it been made for another little girl? Someone like Mara, but long ago? Had she loved playing with her, maybe in a dollhouse of her very own?

The more she looked at the doll, the more she liked her.

"Do you want to come and live in my dollhouse?" she asked Charlotte.

Of course, the doll couldn't answer. Still, Mara imagined she heard a soft whisper in her ear. "Home," said the voice. "Yes."

Mara smiled at the doll. "That's settled, then," she said.

She put the paper in the envelope, and tucked it into Charlotte's pocket. Then Mara closed the cabinet doors and walked back to the front of the store.

"Did you find anything you like?" Mr. Ends asked.

Mara held out the doll. "This one," she said.

Mr. Ends looked at her. "You're very sure?" he asked.

Mara nodded. "I think she's perfect for my house," she said. She pulled some money from her pocket and laid it on the counter.

"Very well, then," said Mr. Ends. "If you're quite certain."

Mara nodded.

Mr. Ends took the doll, wrapped her in white tissue paper, and slipped her into a black box, as if he were putting her to bed. *Or into a coffin*, Mara thought, wondering where such a morbid thought had come from.

"Here you are," Mr. Ends said, handing the box to Mara. "I hope the two of you become the best of friends."

Mara held the box in her hands. "Thanks," she said.

"One thing," said Mr. Ends.

Mara looked at him.

"Every night when you put her to bed, be sure to say this rhyme." Mr. Ends recited in a singsong tone:

"Stay asleep, don't walk around.

Only in your bed be found.

In the morning you can wake,

but all night long stay tucked in safe."

Mara laughed. "What happens if I don't say that?"

"Just remember to say the rhyme every night, and there's nothing at all to worry about," said Mr. Ends.

Jesse came over and pulled on Mara's hand. "Dad's here," he said.

"Don't forget," said Mr. Ends.

"I won't," said Mara. "Bye."

She repeated the words to herself as she and Jesse went outside and got into the car. But by the time they were halfway home, she'd already forgotten them.

"Do you want to read before you go to sleep?"
Mara asked Charlotte.

After dinner, she had finished putting the
last touches on the dollhouse. Then she and
her father had moved it into her bedroom,
where it now sat on a table by the window.

She had decided to put the new resident of
the house in the attic bedroom, mostly because
it was the one she would want to have if she

lived there herself. It took up the whole top floor, and had its own bathroom with a big claw-foot bathtub to take long bubble baths in. There was a round window at one end of the room and the bed faced it, so that a doll could lie there and look out. Mara's mother had even run power to the house, so the lamp on the nightstand turned on.

The bed itself was brass, with a tiny hand-made quilt that Mara's father, who was handy with a needle and thread, had made out of pieces of her favorite clothes that she had outgrown. He had also made a nightgown for Charlotte, white with red ribbons at the wrists and around the neck. She was wearing it now. Her dress was hung up in the wardrobe that stood against one wall.

Mara looked at the little bookcase that occupied one corner of the room, next to a comfortable armchair that a doll could sit in if she wanted to curl up and read. The bookcase was filled with miniature books, copies of some of Mara's favorites. She and her father had made them out of pieces of paper glued together and bound with cloth tape, and Mara had drawn the titles and covers on the fronts to match the ones in her own bookcase. She looked at the row of books, trying to decide which one Charlotte would like best. She selected *Tom's Midnight Garden* by Philippa Pearce.

"This is a really good one," she said to Charlotte. "It's about a boy and a magic clock and a door to a secret garden, only it turns out that it's really all a . . ." She stopped. "Well, I don't want to spoil it for you. You can read it for yourself."

She placed the little book in Charlotte's hands, pulled the quilt up, and left her to read while she got into her own bed and picked up the book she was reading, *Chasing Vermeer* by Blue Balliett. She'd gotten it from the library the Saturday before, and was already halfway through the mystery about a missing painting and the kids trying to find out who stole it. She couldn't wait to find out what happened next.

A few minutes later, her mother appeared in the doorway. She walked over to the dollhouse and looked inside.

"Charlotte looks cozy," she said. "Oh, and I see she's reading a good book." She sat down on the edge of Mara's bed. "I must have read that book to you a thousand times before you could read it for yourself."

"Don't exaggerate," Mara said. "It was probably only two or three *hundred* times."

"Well," her mother said, "it was one of my favorites when I was your age, so I didn't mind one bit. I still remember how surprised I was when I found out who Hatty really was."

"Shh!" Mara warned. "Charlotte just started it."

"Sorry," her mother apologized. She stood up. "Don't stay up too late," she said. "Either of you." She leaned down and gave Mara a kiss. "Good night."

"Night," Mara said.

Her mother left, and Mara went back to reading. Soon after, she yawned and her eyes started to close. Reluctantly, she set the book down and turned out her light. She left the one in the dollhouse on so that she could look at Charlotte reading in her little bed.

"You heard Mom," she said, closing her eyes. "Don't stay up too late."

She drifted off to sleep. What seemed like only a few moments later, she was woken up by the sound of thunder crashing overhead and the whole house shaking. She sat up and looked around. Outside her window, lightning flashed. Rain pattered on the roof.

Mara went to turn on her light, but nothing happened. That's when she realized that the light in the dollhouse was also out. The storm had knocked out the electricity.

Mara wasn't afraid of storms, or the dark. She actually liked them. She enjoyed the sound of rain overhead while she was safe and dry inside. And although the lightning could be a little scary, it was also thrilling to see it light up the world outside and then count the seconds until the thunder answered with its low rumble, letting her know how far away it was.

Besides, she was prepared. She had a flashlight in her bedside table drawer. Sometimes she used it to read under the covers when she was supposed to be asleep. Now she took it out and turned it on. The beam cast a warm glow around her bed.

Mara pointed the light at the dollhouse as another lightning flash crackled outside and the rain fell more fiercely. In the attic, everything seemed okay. Then she realized that Charlotte's bed was empty.

She got up and walked over to the dollhouse. Sure enough, Charlotte wasn't in her bed. The little book she'd been reading was on the floor, and the quilt was turned down. But she wasn't there.

Mara looked on the floor of her own room, thinking perhaps the doll had somehow fallen out of bed. *Maybe the thunder shook the house hard enough to knock her out*, she thought, although she knew this was unlikely.

She shined the light around, looking under the table and around the room. There was no doll. She searched farther out, even looking under her bed. Charlotte wasn't there.

Something moved behind her, and she turned around. Her cat, Gizmo, had jumped up on the table and was sitting there next to the house, watching her as he twitched his tail.

"Hey, Gizmo," Mara said, going over and scratching the cat behind the ears. "Did you knock Charlotte out of bed?"

Gizmo meowed.

"Hmm," Mara said. "Well, if you didn't, then what happened to her?"

Lightning sparked outside, and as it did, Mara caught a glimpse of something white fluttering in the hallway outside her bedroom. Mara pointed her flashlight at the doorway, but nothing was there.

She ran to the door anyway and looked out into the hallway. At the far end, a flash of white disappeared around the corner, in the direction of Jesse's room.

Aha! she thought. *Jesse is trying to scare me by dressing like a ghost with a sheet over his head.*

She wasn't about to be scared by her little brother. She marched down the hallway and went to his room. Opening the door, she said, "Gotcha!"

Jesse was sound asleep in his bed, snoring loudly.

Mara looked around. Jesse really did seem to be asleep, and not pretending. There was no sheet on the floor. She shut the door as quietly as she could and looked around the hallway. Suddenly, she was just the tiniest bit scared. What had she seen?

Thunder shook the house. Mara walked quickly back to her room and got into her bed. She lay in the dark, staring at the empty attic bedroom in the dollhouse. She told herself that she had just seen shadows in the hallway, maybe lightning flashing on the walls. That was all.

Eventually, the storm moved along, leaving only the rain to tap its fingers on the roof. Mara finally fell asleep and dreamed of following someone down a long hallway. She called for the person to stop, but the only reply was the sound of a girl laughing. Mara hurried, trying to catch up, but the person she chased was always just out of reach.

———————

She woke up to Gizmo licking her hair. It had stopped raining, and the morning sun lit up her room. She sat up and looked over at the doll-house. Charlotte was back in her bed.

Mara went over and looked at her. The quilt was pulled up to her chin, and her arms rested on top of them, folded neatly over her chest. Even though the doll's painted-on eyes were open, she seemed to be asleep.

"I guess I dreamed all of that about her being missing," Mara said to Gizmo. "Right?"

Gizmo meowed and licked his paw.

Mara left Charlotte to sleep a little longer, and went downstairs to breakfast. Her father had made blueberry pancakes, and after a couple of bites she'd forgotten all about the weird dream.

4

"These are the best cookies *ever*!" Olivia said, although because her mouth was full it sounded more like, "Deezer de bess cookees evah."

Mara dunked one of the still-warm chocolate chip pistachio orange cookies into her glass of milk and tasted it. Olivia was right. They *were* the best cookies ever. She ate the rest of the cookie in two bites, then picked up another one.

It was Friday, and Olivia was at Mara's house for a sleepover. As they always did when Olivia spent the night, they'd had pizza for dinner, then picked a cookie recipe to try making themselves. Now that the cookies were done, it was time to watch a movie. Mara had chosen the movie last time, so it was Olivia's turn now.

"What DVD did you bring?" Mara asked as they went into the TV room with their plates of cookies and glasses of milk.

Olivia reached into her backpack, which was on the floor by the couch, and pulled out a DVD. "*Unicorn Laser Force: Glittermane's Birthday Surprise*," she said, grinning. "It just came out."

Unicorn Laser Force was Mara and Olivia's favorite show. It was about a team of unicorn astronauts who traveled the galaxy having adventures. This was the first full-length movie about the characters, and Mara had been dying to see it since it was announced months before.

She and Olivia settled into their spots on the couch and turned the movie on. It was just as exciting and fantastic as Mara had hoped it would be. She particularly liked the part where the leader of the Unicorn Laser Force, Sparkles Major, used her laser horn to defeat the evil Gunkbots, who were polluting the oceans of Starsea 7, the home planet of the friendly Merponies. Afterward, the entire crew of the Laser Force ship, the SS *Hoofspeed*, celebrated by throwing a party for Glittermane, the newest recruit, who was sad because it was his first time away from home and he thought nobody knew it was his birthday. They baked him a cake to make him feel welcome, and gave him a box of ribbons for his mane as a present.

"That was awesome," Olivia said when it was over. Then she turned to Mara. "We should throw a birthday party!"

"My birthday was last month," Mara reminded her. "And yours is two months away."

"Not for us," Olivia said. "For your new doll."

"Charlotte?" Mara said.

"Sure," said Olivia. "Kind of a welcome to your new home and birthday all in one. We can make a cake and decorations and everything! Come on. It will be fun."

Mara thought it *did* sound like fun. So they went upstairs to her room and got to work. First, they made a cake out of pink modeling clay and wrote HAPPY BIRTHDAY, CHARLOTTE! on it with a silver glitter pen. They even made little candles out of pieces of white toothpicks painted yellow at the ends to look like flames. Then they wrapped a couple of tiny boxes with scraps of wrapping paper and tied them with ribbon. Finally, they made decorations and a tiny party hat out of construction paper, string, and glitter.

Mara put the hat on Charlotte's head. The cake went on the table in the dollhouse dining room, with the presents piled beside it. Charlotte sat in a chair at the table, looking at the cake and gifts while Mara and Olivia sang "Happy Birthday" to her.

"Blow out the candles and make a wish, Charlotte," Olivia said when they were done. She looked at Mara. "What do you think she wished for?"

"I don't know," Mara said. "What would a doll want?"

"Maybe to be a real person?" Olivia suggested. "Or for another doll to keep her company? She might get lonely being all by herself."

"She's got me," Mara said. "And you know what a good friend I am."

Olivia laughed. "You're the *best* friend," she said. She looked back at the dollhouse. "I wish we could have a sleepover in Charlotte's house. It's so cool."

She reached out and touched Charlotte's hair. "It feels so real," she remarked. She looked at Mara, suddenly very serious. "You know, I heard that they used to make dolls of dead people and use their real hair on them."

"What?" Mara said. "That's so creepy."

Olivia nodded. "Yeah," she said. "And they didn't just use their hair. They would make clothes for the doll out of clothes the real person wore."

Mara looked at the quilt her father had made from her own clothes. "I guess that makes sense," she said. "It's like a way of remembering the person."

"And sometimes the ghost of the dead person would come and live in the doll," Olivia continued, her voice now low and spooky. "And *sometimes* the dolls would come to *life*." She made her eyes wide, pretending to be scared, and waggled her fingers menacingly.

"Very funny," Mara said.

"No, it's true!" Olivia insisted. "In the old days there were haunted dolls all over the place."

"You'd better watch out, or I'll make one of you!" Mara teased.

"You should!" Olivia said. "Then I could live in the dollhouse with Charlotte and have birthday parties every day. Here, you can cut some of my hair to use on it." She held out a length of her long red hair.

Mara picked up a pair of scissors they'd used for cutting out paper and pretended she was going to cut some of Olivia's hair off. Olivia pulled her hair away, and the two of them laughed.

"What's so funny?" Jesse said, poking his head into Mara's room.

Mara snapped the scissors at him. "We're making haunted dolls," she said. "Give us some of your hair!"

Jesse rolled his eyes. "You guys are nuts," he announced.

"Snip! Snip! Snip!" Mara said, walking toward him.

Jesse scampered off as Mara's mother came in. "I hope those aren't my good scissors," she said.

Mara set the scissors down. "Umm, I don't think so," she said, covering them with a sheet of construction paper.

"Hmm," her mother said. "Well, it's time to wrap up the birthday party and get to bed. It's late."

Mara and Olivia changed into their pajamas and brushed their teeth. Then they climbed into Mara's bed. Mara's mother turned out the light, but Mara and Olivia didn't go to sleep right away. They talked for a long time and giggled so much that both Mara's mother *and* father came by to remind them that it was *very* late.

Eventually, they did fall asleep. Mara was having a wonderful dream about traveling to Jupiter with the Unicorn Laser Force when suddenly it was interrupted by the sound of someone singing.

"Happy birthday to me," a girl sang in a voice that was more like a whisper. "Happy birthday to me."

Mara opened her eyes. "Olivia," she said softly. "You're talking in your sleep."

Olivia snorted and rolled over. Mara closed her eyes and tried to get back to her dream.

"Happy birthday to me." The voice came again. "Happy birthday, dear Charlotte. Happy birthday to me."

Mara was wide awake now. She sat up and looked over at the dollhouse. In the moonlight, she could see Charlotte seated at the table in front of her birthday cake, just as they'd left her. Slipping out of bed, Mara walked over and stood in front of the dollhouse.

But not everything looked the way it had before they went to sleep. One of the presents she and Olivia had wrapped was now open. The paper had been torn off and was on the floor of the dollhouse. The ribbon hung off the side of the table. And beside the box was a tiny pair of scissors that looked just like the ones Mara had used. Mara didn't remember there being a pair of scissors in the dollhouse before.

Mara lifted up the piece of construction paper on her own table. The scissors were gone. She looked back at the dollhouse and noticed something else on the table that hadn't been there the night before. Lying beside the scissors was what looked like a lock of dark hair.

Mara's hand instinctively went to her own hair. On the left side, it felt normal. Mara let out a sigh of relief. But then as her hand went to the right side, her breath caught. A big piece was missing.

5

"I didn't do it!"

Jesse stamped his foot and scowled at Mara, who stood in his room with her hands on her hips, scowling back.

"Then who did?" Mara asked crossly. After discovering that her hair had been cut, she'd been unable to go back to sleep, lying in bed and wondering how it had happened. Now she was tired and angry.

Jesse shrugged. "What about Olivia?"

Mara hesitated. Of course she had asked Olivia. And Olivia had seemed genuinely shocked to see what had happened. Mara believed her when she said she hadn't done it. But she also really didn't think that Jesse would do something so mean either. Still, *someone* had done it, and they were the only two possibilities.

"Olivia would never do something like this," she said.

"So, you believe her but not me?" Jesse said. He looked like he was about to cry.

"What's going on?" Mara's father asked as he and her mother walked into the room.

"Somebody"—she stared hard at Jesse—"cut my hair while I was sleeping," Mara said. "Look at it!"

Her father looked at the place where her hair used to be. Then he looked at Jesse too.

"I told her, I didn't do it!" Jesse insisted.

Mara's mother ran her hands through Mara's hair. "If we restyle it a little, you won't even be able to tell," she said unconvincingly.

"I look ridiculous!" Mara wailed. She pointed at her brother. "I know you did it. You heard Olivia and me talking about using hair to make dolls."

"I did not!" Jesse shouted. "I don't care about stupid dolls, and I wouldn't touch your stupid hair if you *paid* me!"

"Okay," Mara's mother said. "I think you both need a little time to cool down. Mara, let's go to your room."

Mara shot Jesse one last nasty look as her mother put her arm around her shoulders and marched her out of the room. Jesse stuck his tongue out at her in response.

Mara and her mother went back to Mara's room, where Olivia was sitting on the edge of the bed, looking worried. Mara sat down next to her.

"Mara, do you really think Jesse cut your hair?" Mara's mother asked.

"Who else could have done it?" said Mara. "I know Olivia didn't."

"Could you have done it yourself?" her mother asked. "Maybe in your sleep without realizing it?"

"You mean like sleepwalking?" said Mara.

"We *were* talking about cutting our hair right before we went to bed," Olivia said. "Maybe you dreamed about it and actually did it. That happened to me once. I dreamed

I was picking blueberries and eating them, and then I woke up and realized I was standing in the kitchen eating the blueberry pie my grandmother had brought us all the way from Maine. I'd eaten almost half of it and didn't even know it."

"I guess maybe I could have done it," Mara said.

Although she said it, she didn't really believe it. For one thing, if she had done it, where was the big chunk of hair that was cut off? And how could she explain the tiny scissors in the dollhouse, or the little lock of hair she'd found there? Still, she didn't say anything. It would sound too weird, and she had already upset everyone enough.

"I think maybe you owe Jesse an apology," her mother said gently.

Mara sighed. She got up and went back to Jesse's room, where she found him and their father putting together a LEGO castle. Jesse was laughing and smiling, but when he saw Mara, he frowned.

"Sorry," Mara muttered.

Jesse shrugged. "It's okay."

Mara turned around and returned to her room. At breakfast a little while later, Jesse seemed to have forgotten the whole thing. Mara wished she could forget it too, but every time she pushed her hair away from her face, she remembered that a chunk of it was missing. Then she got mad all over again.

Olivia left after breakfast to run errands with her mother, and Mara went back up to her room. She walked over to the dollhouse. Charlotte was still seated at the table with the cake and the presents in front of her. The pair of scissors and the lock of hair were there too. Mara picked the scissors up. The house was filled with all kinds of miniature things: rolling pins, a sewing machine, plates, footstools, plants, even pots and pans for the kitchen. Maybe there had been a pair of scissors in there all along and Mara had simply forgotten about it.

But she didn't think so.

Mara put the scissors back on the table and went to her mother's office on the third floor. Her mother was at her drafting table, working.

"Can I look something up on the computer?" Mara asked.

"Of course," her mother said.

Mara sat at the desk, clicked on the mouse that sat on a pad there, and went to an online search engine. She typed some words and waited to see what results came up. Then she scanned the list of pages and chose one to visit. When it loaded, she started reading.

The practice of making death dolls (sometimes called memorial dolls) is an ancient one, found in many cultures around the world. The dolls are made to resemble the deceased person, and may incorporate the dead person's hair, bones, or teeth. Dolls may be dressed in clothing similar to what the person wore in life, and accessories representing their professions or interests may be fashioned for them.

Of particular interest is the work of Violeta Grundy (1878–1952), a dollmaker who lived in the Allegheny Mountains of Appalachia.

Grundy made numerous dolls for clients who sought her out for her ability to capture the likenesses of the dead in her creations. She worked primarily in cloth, wood, and sometimes ceramics, and her dolls were all inscribed with her initials somewhere on the body.

There were several photographs with the article, showing some of the dolls created by Violeta Grundy. Mara looked at them closely, especially the ones showing her initials scratched into the bodies.

"Did you find what you were looking for?" her mother asked from behind her.

"Um, sort of," Mara said. "I mean maybe."

Her mother leaned over and peered at the screen. "Researching dolls?" she asked.

Mara fumbled with the mouse, closing the window before her mother could see the part about the dolls being haunted.

"Yeah," she said. "I was just curious about where Charlotte might have come from." She got up. "Thanks for letting me use the computer." Mara left the office.

She went back to her room and over to the dollhouse. She picked up Charlotte, placing her tiny birthday hat on the table.

"Sorry about this," she said as she lifted up Charlotte's dress and turned her upside down. "I know it's rude."

At first, she didn't see anything. But then she noticed it—on Charlotte's lower back, there were two small letters. A *V* and a *G* were engraved onto her porcelain skin.

"Violeta Grundy," Mara said, turning Charlotte right side up again and smoothing out her dress. She sighed. She almost wished she hadn't found the initials. If there'd been nothing there, she would have been able to keep thinking of Charlotte as an ordinary doll, and of the weird things that were happening as coincidences.

But now she knew that Charlotte had been made by someone known for creating dolls that represented people who had died. She looked at Charlotte's face. "I know what you are," she said. "Now I just have to figure out *who* you are."

6

On Saturday night, Mara's parents had tickets to the ballet, and Mara and Jesse had a babysitter. Her name was Carolina North. She was sixteen, lived down the street, and had been their babysitter since she was thirteen. Mara and Jesse liked her because of her funny name and because she was not quite as tough about enforcing their parents' rules as she probably ought to have been.

Not that she was irresponsible. She made them do their homework (if they had any) and even helped them with it. She made sure they ate dinner before they ate dessert. But she let them watch things their parents might not entirely approve of if they knew, and sometimes she let bedtime go by without telling them to brush their teeth and put their pajamas on.

On this particular night, Mara and Jesse had no homework to do, although Mara had spent all day thinking about Violeta Grundy and her dolls, and wished she could find more information on them. But her parents had a strict no-computer rule when they weren't home, and that was one thing Carolina always stuck to.

Instead, they were watching a horror movie. And it just happened to be a movie about a stuffed clown that came to life and terrorized a group of kids having a sleepover. Jesse thought it was great, even though it would probably give him nightmares, but Mara could only watch about twenty minutes of it before she pretended to yawn and said she was really tired and thought she would go to bed.

Once she got to her room, she realized that she *was* really tired. She and Olivia had stayed up way past their normal bedtime the night before, and now it was getting late again. So when Mara got into bed, it didn't take her long to fall asleep.

She woke up when she heard the grandfather clock in the downstairs hall chiming. Its big voice boomed through the house like a giant calling the hour: *Bong! Bong! Bong!*

Although she was still half asleep, Mara found herself counting along with the clock. When it reached twelve, she thought it must be done. But then it clanged one more time.

Thirteen? she thought. *How funny. Just like the clock in* Tom's Midnight Garden.

She rolled over and stretched. Her hands touched something cool and metallic. She felt around again. It was the headboard of her bed. Only her headboard was made of wood, and this was metal.

She sat up and reached for the lamp on her bedside table. But instead of a switch, her fingers touched a string. She pulled it and the light came on.

She was not in her own bed. She was in a brass bed. And when she looked down, she wasn't wearing her pajamas; she was wearing a white nightgown with red ribbon at the wrists and neck. She was in a different room than the one she'd gone to sleep in.

She was in the attic of the dollhouse.

It took a moment for this fact to sink in, because it was too weird to be true. But it was. The bed was the one in the attic bedroom. The quilt covering the bed was the one her father had made, and so was the nightgown she was wearing. She had painted the trim in the room herself.

At first, she thought she must be dreaming. But she felt very much awake. She touched the bedspread again, and the bedside table. They were real too.

She got out of bed and stepped onto the wood boards of the floor. They were cool beneath her bare feet. She walked around, looking at everything. There was the dresser, the braided rug, the mirror. All the miniature things she had put into the bedroom of the dollhouse. Only now they were all life-sized.

Moonlight was coming in through the large window at the end of the room. Mara walked over to it and looked out. But instead of seeing trees, or a lawn, or anything she might expect to see out the window of a house, she saw her own bedroom. What she had thought was moonlight was the glow of the lamp on her bedside table.

Before she could even begin to comprehend what was happening, something blocked out the light. Suddenly, a huge brown eye appeared in the window. It stared at her, unblinking, as she stared back, her heart thumping in her chest. She stepped away from the window, horrified.

The eye retreated, and Mara rushed to the glass. Outside, a face came into view. She saw pale skin, rosy cheeks, a red mouth. Now two eyes stared back at her, both open wide.

It was Charlotte.

The doll stood in Mara's room. Charlotte was wearing her red dress, and looked exactly as she always did. Only she was enormous, a giant who towered over the house as she looked at it with eyes that never blinked.

But it's not just that Charlotte's big, Mara realized. *I'm small.*

Charlotte turned away from the house and walked stiffly out of Mara's bedroom. Where was she going? Mara thought about Jesse, who was probably asleep in his own room. Were their parents home yet? Or was Carolina still there? Then Mara remembered the clock striking thirteen. That was impossible, of course. And yet, she had counted the chimes.

She turned and ran down the dollhouse staircase from the attic to the second floor. There were bedrooms here, all of them empty except for the furniture Mara had put into them. She ran down another flight and found herself in the front hall of the house. There was the grandfather clock she had heard. She had helped her mother put it together from a kit. But that one had been fake. This one was real. The hands were slowly circling the dial, but they were going backward.

Mara ran into the dining room, where she found the table covered with presents. The party hat that Charlotte had been wearing was there. Next to it lay a doll. A doll with brown hair and smooth brown skin. A doll that looked a lot like Mara. She picked it up. It had been made out of some of the clay from which she and Olivia had fashioned the birthday cake. And on its head was real hair. Her hair.

Mara dropped the doll in horror and spun around. It was then that she realized that where there should have been no wall, there now was one. She should have been able to look out into her room. Instead, she was staring at a wall. The dollhouse had somehow transformed into an actual house.

And she was trapped inside it.

7

Mara ran to the front door of the dollhouse and tried to open it. The knob wouldn't budge. She pulled and twisted it, but it was stuck fast. She banged her fists on the door until they hurt, but it remained closed. She even thought about kicking it, but she was barefoot, and she knew she would only injure herself.

Next she tried the windows. None of them would open. She ran from one to the next, pulling back the curtains and trying to get the latches to turn. They were all frozen in place. Outside the window lay her bedroom, but all she could do was look at it. Charlotte had turned off the light when she left the room, and everything was now in shadow. All she could see was her bed, her dresser, and the door to the hallway.

Not knowing what else to do, Mara walked through the downstairs of the house. In the kitchen, the taps didn't run and the food in the refrigerator was all fake. The piano in the parlor didn't make any music when she touched the keys, and the goldfish in the bowl on a stand in the library was stuck in place, swimming nowhere.

Only the grandfather clock was working. The hands were still moving backward, and Mara wondered what that meant. Was time itself going backward? Or was it all part of whatever magic had caused her and Charlotte to switch places?

She climbed the stairs back to the bedroom in the attic. She sat down on the bed and picked up the copy of *Tom's Midnight Garden* that she had made for Charlotte to read. Like everything else in the house, it wasn't real either. There was no printing on the pages, no illustrations inside. It was just paper and glue and tape.

Nothing around her felt real. It all *looked* real, but it wasn't. Food was cardboard and plastic. The bathtub could never be filled with water. Yes, some of the lights turned on, thanks to her mother's ingenuity. But that almost made it worse. Things looked like they should work, but they didn't. She couldn't believe she'd ever thought it would be fun to live in the dollhouse. Not like this, anyway.

She curled up on the bed. At least that was more or less comfortable. And the quilt her father had made was real. She wrapped herself up in it and tried to figure out what to do. She couldn't get out of the house through the usual ways. And even if she could, what would she do? She was so small now that Gizmo would probably think she was a mouse and eat her.

She started to cry. Then she picked up the phony copy of *Tom's Midnight Garden* and threw it across the room. As she did, an envelope fell out and fluttered to the floor. Mara, sniffling, got up and retrieved it. She sat back down on the bed and opened it. As soon as she saw what was written on the paper inside, she knew what it was—the letter she had discovered in the pocket of Charlotte's dress the day she had found her in the shop. Before, it had been too tiny to read. Now it wasn't.

My Dear Charlotte:

I do not know why you were taken from me so soon. My heart is broken at the loss of you. But there is still hope. I will fashion a doll, the most beautiful doll I have yet made. I will make for it a dress like the one you longed for in life, scarlet, like the fever that claimed you. I will give it your hair. I know that someday we will be reunited in the Hereafter. Until then, you will live with me in this form.

Your Loving Mother,
Violeta Grundy

Mara read the letter a second time, trying to understand it. Then she folded it and set it on the bedside table. She still wasn't sure what exactly was happening, but now she had a better idea. Violeta had made a doll of her dead daughter, Charlotte. That much was clear now. But how had Charlotte come to life? And how had she switched places with Mara?

Most importantly, how could Mara get her to switch back?

Mara thought hard. She was good at puzzles, and this was a puzzle. She just had to figure out what all the pieces were and how they fit together. She sat on the bed and tried to remember everything that had happened since she'd bought Charlotte at the shop.

First, she had thought she'd seen someone walking in the hallway. Could that have been

Charlotte? And could it possibly have been Charlotte who had cut her hair while she was asleep? A day or two ago, that would have seemed ridiculous. Now it seemed like the most obvious answer. Somehow, Charlotte was coming alive at night and getting out of the dollhouse and into the real world.

And now she had trapped Mara inside the dollhouse. Mara remembered the weird clay doll sitting on the table in the dining room. Obviously, it was supposed to be her. That's why Charlotte had needed her hair.

Then Mara remembered something else. The strange man at the shop—Odson Ends— had told her to say a rhyme every night after putting Charlotte to bed. Mara had thought it was silly and hadn't done it. Could that really be why Charlotte had come to life? Because she hadn't said the rhyme? It seemed ridiculous. But there was no other explanation.

Mara struggled to recall the words Odson Ends had recited.

"Stay asleep, don't walk around," she said aloud. "I remember that was how it started. But what was the rest?"

She could remember a few words and phrases—*wake*, *all night long*, *safe*—but not the whole thing. Now she wished she had written it down. Even more, she wished she had said it like she was supposed to. If she had, then maybe none of this would be happening.

She wondered what Charlotte was doing. Was she walking around Mara's house? What would happen if someone saw her? She half hoped someone would. Even then, though, they wouldn't know to look for Mara in the dollhouse. And what would they do if they found her?

She tried to imagine being this size forever. What if she had to live in the dollhouse for the rest of her life? It was such a strange thing to even think about. Part of her thought that she must be dreaming everything that was happening. That it was *really* happening was just too bizarre to believe.

Her thoughts were interrupted by the clanging of the grandfather clock. Suddenly, the room around Mara seemed to dim. The shadows lengthened. She had only a moment to be frightened before she found herself surrounded by dark shapes that seemed to rush toward her.

Mara squeezed her eyes shut and screamed.

"Mara!" A familiar voice broke through her own.

Mara stopped screaming and opened her eyes. She was sitting in her own bed, wearing her own pajamas. Rain pattered against the window, and her father was standing in the doorway of her room, a startled expression on his face and a mug of coffee in his hand.

"What's wrong?" he asked.

"Bad dream," she said. "I'm okay now." She couldn't tell him that she had been trapped in the dollhouse. He would think she was crazy. This was something she was going to have to figure out on her own.

"You sure?"

She was not at all sure, but she nodded.

"Okay," her father said. "Well, breakfast will be ready in fifteen."

He left, and Mara immediately leaped out of bed and ran to the dollhouse. Charlotte was lying in her bed, staring at the ceiling with her painted-on eyes that never closed. Mara was tempted to pick the doll up and throw her away, or try to destroy her. But she had a feeling that would just make things worse. She had to find another way to stop what was happening. And she knew where she had to start.

It was time to go back to Frightville.

8

Mara pedaled her bike through the rain.

She wasn't supposed to ride as far as she was going, but this was an emergency. And she hadn't wanted to ask her parents to drive her to Frightville because she knew that if she did, she would tell them everything about what was happening. Then they would think she had gone crazy, or had a fever that was making her imagine things, and would either make her lie down or take her to see Dr. Herren.

She didn't need a doctor. She needed someone who could tell her what kind of magic was bringing Charlotte to life. More important than that, she needed someone who could tell her how to stop it.

The rain started to fall harder, as if it didn't want Mara to get where she was going. It pattered on her red raincoat and ran into her eyes. Her hair was already soaking wet, as were her sneakers, and she was going to have a lot of explaining to do when she got home later.

She hoped Frightville was even open. The store had no website, and she'd been unable to find out what its hours were. Since it was Sunday, there was a good chance it wasn't open at all.

Her worst fear was confirmed when she brought her bike to a stop in front of the shop and saw a CLOSED sign hanging in the window of the front door. She went to the door anyway, pressing her face to the glass and trying to see inside. But all the lights were off, and nobody was in there.

"Are you here for the gathering, dear?" asked a voice behind her.

Mara turned around. Standing there was a pair of women who were obviously twins. Very, very odd-looking twins. They were quite old—Mara guessed they were eighty at *least*—and quite short. Both were dressed in black dresses with black shawls around their shoulders. Their hair was frizzy and gray, and looked as if it hadn't been combed in years. One of them held the handle of a large purple umbrella, which spread out over their heads and kept the rain off.

"Um, no," Mara said. "I wanted to talk to the man who owns the shop."

"Odson," one of the twins said. "He's our very dear friend."

"We are Persimmon and Pawpaw Porridge," the other twin said, not saying which of them was which.

"I'm Mara," said Mara.

"May I ask what you wish to speak to Odson about?" asked the left-hand twin.

Mara hesitated. She didn't know the women at all, apart from their names, and she didn't know what kind of help they could be to her anyway.

"I should probably speak to Mr. Ends," she said.

The right-hand twin sighed. "I'm afraid he's gone away on a buying trip," she said. "He's letting us use the magic—"

"He's letting us use the back room of the shop," the left-hand twin interrupted. She gave her sister a stern look. "For our little get-together."

"Oh," Mara said. "When will he be back?"

"Next Thursday, I believe," said the right-hand twin.

Mara sighed. The rain started to fall harder.

"Perhaps we should continue our conversation inside," said the left-hand twin. She produced a key from her pocket and inserted it into the lock of the door, opening it.

The twins entered the shop, and Mara followed them. One of the women turned on the lights, and the warm glow made Mara feel a little better. But only a little.

"Now then," said one of the twins. "What was it you needed to speak to Odson about? My sister and I might be able to help you. We're quite experienced with things of this nature." She gestured her hand around, as if she were talking about the items in the shop.

"Okay," Mara said. "Well, I bought this doll here the other day. Mr. Ends told me I was supposed to say a rhyme every night when I put her to bed. Only I forgot and—"

"You forgot!" both the twins said, gasping in unison.

Mara nodded. "And now . . ." She didn't know how to finish the sentence, so she just shrugged.

The twins looked at each other. "And now things have become peculiar," the left-hand twin said.

"*Very* peculiar," said Mara.

She wondered how the twins knew about the rhyme, and if they knew about Charlotte's story. Before she could ask, they started talking to each other.

"I knew it was a bad idea for Odson to put Violeta's—" said one.

"We *warned* him," said the other.

"Well, I hope it's not too late," the first added.

"Too late?" Mara said. "Too late for what?"

The twins looked at her as if they'd forgotten that she was there.

"Never you mind," said the right-hand twin. "It's all going to be fine. We know *just* what to do."

"Well, we know what *you* need to do," the other interjected.

"What?" Mara asked.

The twins looked at each other again. This time, they looked very serious.

"You have to convince her to move on," the left-hand twin said.

"Move on?" said Mara. "You mean like out of the dollhouse?"

The twins shook their heads.

"Not like that," said the right-hand twin. "Move on to the Hereafter."

"The Hereafter," Mara said. "Violeta said something about that in her letter."

Now the twins switched from shaking to nodding.

"Yes," said the left-hand twin. "You need to tell her that her mother is waiting for her in the Hereafter. Tell her that they need to be reunited."

"That sounds easy enough," said Mara. "I mean, why wouldn't she want to be reunited with her mother?"

Both twins sighed sadly.

"Ghosts aren't like us, dear," said the right-hand twin. "They're something in-between. They remember what it was to be human, and they long for that again."

"So, how do I convince Charlotte to go?" Mara asked.

"You'll need to talk to her," the left-hand twin answered.

"Sure," Mara said. "But how? It's not like she's alive all the time. It only happens at night."

The twins nodded once again. "Yes," said the right-hand one. "That's when it happens. I'm guessing there's a clock involved?"

"The grandfather clock," Mara said. "In the dollhouse. The hands were moving backward."

"You'll need to stop the clock," the left-hand twin explained.

"But don't break it!" the right-hand twin warned. "If you break the clock, you'll be stuck in the dollhouse forever. You just need to stop it for a short time. That will bring Charlotte back into the house with you."

"And then you can talk to her," the left-hand twin concluded.

Mara sighed. This was sounding more and more difficult.

"I'm sure you can do it, dear," said the right-hand twin.

"I hope so," Mara said. She looked at them. "But what if I can't?"

The twins smiled, but they weren't convincing.

"Let's hope that doesn't happen," the left-hand one said.

"How do you know so much about Violeta?" Mara asked.

"Would you look at the time?" the right-hand twin said. "I'm afraid we really need to be getting ready, dear."

"Please come back again," the left-hand twin said as she herded Mara toward the door. "When this business is all over."

"Oh," Mara said as she was practically

pushed out into the rain. "Sure. And, um, thank you."

"Don't mention it," the twin seeing her out said. "To anyone."

The strange old woman shut the door, and Mara heard the lock click shut. She waved goodbye, but the twins had already retreated to the back of the store. Mara got on her bicycle and started the long ride home.

She had a feeling it was going to be a very strange night.

"I think you're getting a fever."

Mara's mother placed the back of her hand on Mara's forehead. Mara was sitting on the couch, wrapped in her fuzzy bathrobe and drinking a mug of cocoa.

"I'm warm because I just got out of the shower and now I'm drinking hot chocolate," Mara said.

"I still don't know what possessed you to go riding around in the rain," her mother said.

Mara had hoped to sneak back into the house and get changed into dry clothes before anybody saw her. Unfortunately, she'd come in right as her mother was walking through the kitchen.

Mara didn't say anything. She didn't want to lie, and she couldn't tell the truth. Instead, she faked a sneeze and said, "Maybe you're right."

"I think you should go to bed," her mother said. "With a little luck, you won't get really sick and have to stay home from school tomorrow."

Mara was only too happy to escape to her bedroom. Once she was there, she climbed into bed and thought about what she was going to do. The Porridge Sisters had said she needed to convince Charlotte to move on to the Hereafter. That wasn't much to go on.

For one thing, Mara didn't even know if she would get sucked into the dollhouse again that night. And if she was, she had to somehow stop the grandfather clock without breaking it, which *maybe* would keep Charlotte from leaving the dollhouse and entering Mara's world. Only then could she begin to try to talk to Charlotte. That was a lot of *if*s and *maybe*s.

She couldn't help but look at the dollhouse. Charlotte was still lying in her own bed. Mara hadn't moved her at all. She was a little afraid to touch the doll now that she knew that, supposedly, Charlotte's ghost was inside it. That thought creeped her out.

———

A little while later, her mother came in carrying a tray.

"Your father made your favorite," she said. "Tomato soup and a grilled cheese sandwich."

She set the tray down on Mara's lap. In addition to the food, there was a glass of water and a little glass bottle that looked suspiciously like the one Dr. Herren had prescribed the last time she'd had a fever.

"It can't hurt," her mother said, seeing her eyeing the bottle. "And the pharmacist added bubble-gum flavoring, so no complaining about the taste."

It wasn't the taste Mara was worried about.

She remembered from the last time that the medicine made her sleepy. As her mother poured some of the pink-colored medicine into a spoon, Mara said, "I think I feel a lot better."

"Well, just in case," her mother said, holding out the spoon.

Mara reluctantly opened her mouth. Her mother popped the spoon in, and Mara swallowed. She made a face.

"Eat some soup," her mother said, handing her the soup spoon. "I'll come back in a bit for the tray."

Mara took a sip of the soup. It was delicious, and she realized that she was really hungry. She picked up one half of the sandwich, dunked it into the soup, and took a bite. She quickly ate the whole thing, then started on the other half. Then she finished the soup, scraping the last bits up with the spoon. She was licking off the last drops when her mother came back.

"Well, your appetite certainly isn't sick," her mother joked, taking the tray.

Mara yawned, suddenly sleepy.

"And it looks like the medicine is kicking in too," her mother said. "Why don't you try to sleep now."

"Just a second," Mara said as her mother started to leave.

Her mother turned around. "Can I get the patient anything else?"

"How do you stop a clock?" Mara asked. "You know, like a grandfather clock. One that winds up."

"What a funny question," her mother said. "What made you think about that?"

"*Tom's Midnight Garden*," Mara said. "I was reading it again, and I was wondering what would have happened if Tom stopped the clock from chiming thirteen."

"Hmm," her mother said thoughtfully. "Well, clocks like that have a weight inside that drops, making the gears turn. When it reaches the end of its chain, it has to be wound back up to keep the clock working. If you stopped the weight from falling, that would stop the clock."

"Thanks," Mara said. She yawned again and settled into her pillows.

Her mother left. Mara tried to keep her eyes open, but they kept shutting. Eventually, she gave in and decided to shut them, but just for a little while.

It wasn't until she heard the grandfather clock chiming that she woke up and remembered that she had to stop it before it struck thirteen.

She stumbled out of bed. As soon as she felt the floorboards beneath her feet, she knew she was back in the dollhouse. She didn't know how many times the clock had chimed already, so she ran down the stairs to the hallway as quickly as she could.

She opened the tall front door of the clock and peered inside. Behind the pendulum she could see the weight that controlled the gears. She waited for the pendulum to swing by, then thrust her hand inside and pulled the weight as hard as she could. The chain played out as she dragged the weight down, and there was an alarming grinding sound from inside the clock. The pendulum stopped.

Mara looked at the clock face. The hands

had ceased moving. But had she actually accomplished anything, or had she just broken the clock? She recalled the twins' warning about how she might be trapped there forever if she had.

"Why am I still here?" asked a voice from behind her.

Mara turned around. Charlotte was there, staring at her with her painted-on eyes. She still looked like a doll, but she was obviously alive. She was wearing the red dress.

"You're the girl," Charlotte said. "The one who chose me. The one my mother said would come." Her painted lips didn't move, and her voice seemed to come from far away.

"Yes," Mara said. "I found you in a shop."

Charlotte took a step toward her, and Mara stepped back, afraid.

"Why are you frightened?" Charlotte asked.

"Because you want to trade places with me," said Mara. "And I don't want to live in this house."

"Why not?" Charlotte asked. "It's a lovely house."

"Thank you," said Mara. "My mother and I made it together."

"Mother," Charlotte said, as if she were tasting the word. "I miss my mother."

"I know," Mara said. "I want to talk to you about that. Your mother needs you to go to her. In the Hereafter."

"Hereafter," said Charlotte. She sounded sad. "No. I want to be here. In the real world. In a real house. With my real mother."

"That's the thing," Mara said. "If you stay here, then I have to stay here in this house, and I can't be with *my* mother. Or my father or brother. And that would make me very sad."

Charlotte didn't say anything. Mara wasn't sure what else to say to her to make her understand. Suddenly, she felt very tired. She found herself sitting down on the floor and leaning back against the wall. She put her hand to her forehead. She was burning up.

"Are you ill?" Charlotte's voice was a mix of curiosity and concern.

"I have a fever," Mara said. "That's all. I need to lie down."

"Fever," Charlotte said. She sounded afraid now.

Then Mara remembered—Charlotte had died from scarlet fever.

The doll walked stiffly over to where Mara was slumped against the wall. She bent over and placed a hand on Mara's cheek. The porcelain was cool against Mara's skin.

"I need to lie down," Mara whispered, her voice hoarse. She coughed. "I need my mother. She can help me."

She was feeling really sick now. The fever seemed to be coursing through her. She grew dizzy.

The next thing she knew, she was being picked up. She could feel the hard porcelain of Charlotte's limbs holding her up. The doll was carrying her.

"Where are you taking me?" she asked.

Charlotte replied with one word. Her voice filled Mara's head, like the sound of rain: "Mother."

"Wake up."

Mara heard the voice calling to her. She opened her eyes. A woman she didn't know was bent over her, looking down with concern. When she saw Mara blink, she smiled.

"Ah," she said. "The fever has broken. She's going to be fine."

"Who are you?" Mara asked.

She looked around. She wasn't in her own bedroom. She was in the attic bedroom of the dollhouse. Then she noticed Charlotte standing beside the bed. Only she no longer looked like a doll. She looked like a real girl, with long dark hair and creamy skin.

Charlotte smiled at Mara. "You were right," she said. "Mother was waiting."

Mara looked back at the woman, who was regarding her with a look of contentment. "Violeta?" Mara said.

The woman nodded. "I knew someday my child would return to me," she said.

Mara's mind buzzed with a dozen different thoughts, all of them terrifying. If Violeta was here and Charlotte was no longer a doll, what did that mean?

"Are you . . . ghosts?" Mara asked.

Violeta laughed. "Does it matter what we are?" she replied. "We're together now, and you're no longer ill. That's all that's important."

"No!" Mara said, shaking her head. "I don't want to be a ghost, or a spirit, or whatever. I want to be a real girl, and I want to be in my own house with my own family."

She tried to get out of bed, but Violeta reached out and pushed her back with a firm hand that definitely did not feel like it belonged to a ghost. Mara slapped at her hand. "Stop it! Let me go!"

Violeta frowned. "Perhaps I was too hasty in my diagnosis," she said. "I think the fever still consumes her."

"I'm *fine*," Mara insisted.

Charlotte came over and sat down on the

bed beside her. "It's all right," she said. "We can be sisters now."

"I don't want a sister," Mara said. "I have a brother, and I want to be with him."

Charlotte looked sad. Her mother reached out and placed a hand on her shoulder. "Don't worry, child," Violeta said. "She'll come to like it here with us. In time."

Time. The word stuck in Mara's mind. *Time*. The clock. She had kept Charlotte from leaving the dollhouse by stopping the clock from running backward. Then, somehow, Charlotte had brought the spirit of her mother here to live too. Now they wanted Mara to join their ghost family.

The Porridge Sisters had warned her about breaking the clock and trapping herself in the dollhouse forever. But maybe they were wrong.

Maybe if she stopped the clock altogether, whatever magic was bringing Charlotte and the dollhouse to life would end.

Or maybe they're right and it will mean you're never getting back, Mara thought.

She needed to try. She wasn't ready to become a part of a ghost family, and it was the only thing she could think of. But that meant getting away from Violeta and Charlotte.

"You might be right," she said, trying to sound as if she'd suddenly changed her mind. "It *is* nice here. And it would be fun to have a sister."

Charlotte smiled. "I know so many games," she said. "We're going to be very good friends."

Mara looked at Violeta. "I'll be right back," she said as she pulled aside the quilt. "I need to, um, visit the bathroom."

She got out of bed and padded across the room. When she got to the bathroom, she looked behind her to see if she was being watched. But Violeta and Charlotte had their backs to her.

Mara darted down the stairs. She went as quickly as she could, trying not to make any noise, but her feet thumped on the boards as she ran. She dashed down the second-floor hallway and almost tumbled down the next flight of stairs as she made her way to the first floor. By the time she reached the grandfather clock, she was out of breath and had to stop.

"I hope you're not trying to leave us," called Violeta's voice.

Mara looked up and saw the ghostly form of Charlotte's mother materialize in the hallway.

The air shimmered around her as she became more solid.

"Charlotte will be most disappointed if you leave," Violeta said coldly.

"Yes," said Charlotte. "Most disappointed."

Mara whirled around and saw Charlotte standing behind her. She frowned at Mara. "You're not being a very good friend," she said.

Violeta started to walk toward Mara as Charlotte advanced from the other side. Mara was trapped between them. Her heart pounded, and a scream rose in her throat. She pushed it down and turned to the grandfather clock.

"I won't stay here!" she shouted as she grabbed the clock by the sides.

She pulled. The clock was heavy, and Mara had to use all her strength to budge it. She pulled again, and it leaned forward.

"No!" Violeta said, reaching out toward her.

Mara gave another pull, and the clock toppled. She darted out of the way as it fell, backing into Charlotte.

The clock hit the hallway floor with a crash. Glass shattered, and metal gears poured out. Mara heard a ghostly voice whisper sadly in her ear, "Goodbye, sister." She felt a cold wind tickle her skin.

Then she was standing in her own bedroom.

She looked around. Had she really done it? Had she escaped from the dollhouse and sent Charlotte and her mother into the Hereafter? She looked at the dollhouse. Inside the house's front hall, the little grandfather clock lay in pieces. Mara searched for Charlotte, but the doll was nowhere to be found. The house was empty.

The light in Mara's room went on, and Mara turned to see her mother in the doorway.

"Are you okay?" her mother asked. "I thought I heard you shout."

For a moment, Mara was confused. Was it morning already? She felt as if she'd been inside the dollhouse for only a short time. Maybe she was still dreaming. Maybe it wasn't over yet after all.

"Mara?" her mother said. "Is everything all right? You look like you've seen a ghost."

Mara looked at her window. Outside, the sun was up, spilling warm light across the floor. It really was over. Mara ran to her mother and threw her arms around her, hugging her tightly. "I love you so much," she said.

Her mother patted her hair. "And I love you more," she said. Then she put her hand on

Mara's forehead. "Your fever seems to be gone."

Mara let go. "I feel a lot better," she said.

"I guess you'll be going to school, then," said her mother. "Better get going. Your dad and Jesse are already having breakfast."

Mara had never been so happy to get ready for school. She got dressed in record time, and when she went into the kitchen, she kissed her father on the cheek and gave Jesse a squeeze before she sat down.

"What's gotten into you?" Jesse asked suspiciously as he munched his scrambled eggs.

"Can't I be happy to see my family?" Mara answered, pouring herself some orange juice.

Jesse looked at their father. "You should probably take her to Dr. Herren," he said. "I think she's still sick."

Mara's good mood only got better when she saw what a beautiful day it was. The rain was gone, and the skies were blue and clear. There was a cool, crisp feeling to the morning, and to celebrate she wore her favorite red scarf.

By the time her father dropped her and Jesse off at school, Mara was pretty much convinced that life was back to normal. She would have to explain the broken clock in the dollhouse and why Charlotte was missing, but that wasn't a big deal. If she had to, she would blame it on Gizmo and then make it up to him by buying him a new catnip mouse. Then she would find the most ordinary, non-haunted doll she could find to live in the attic bedroom.

In homeroom she sat next to Olivia, who told her all about the new Unicorn Laser Force comic book she'd gotten at the mall. Mara didn't even mind that she was spoiling the ending for Mara, who hadn't read it yet. She was so happy to be with her friends, having a normal day, that nothing could make her upset.

Ms. Taggart walked in, and Mara wouldn't even have cared if she'd announced a pop quiz on something Mara knew absolutely nothing about. But she didn't. Instead, she said, "Class, I have a special announcement. We have a new student joining us."

Mara looked at Olivia and grinned. A new student was always fun. It meant someone else to do things with.

Then the door opened. All heads turned to see who the new addition to the class was. In the doorway stood a girl. A girl with pale skin, long dark hair, and big brown eyes. Mara had to stop herself from grabbing Olivia's hand.

"Everyone, this is Charlotte," Ms. Taggart said as the new girl walked in and stood in front of the class. "Let's give her a big Crowleyville welcome."

"Hi, Charlotte!" everyone called out. Everyone except Mara.

Charlotte gave a little wave. Her eyes looked around the room. When she settled on Mara, Charlotte smiled.

"Hi," she said. "It's nice to be here. I'm sure we're all going to be very good friends."

ANOTHER SCARE, IF YOU DARE!

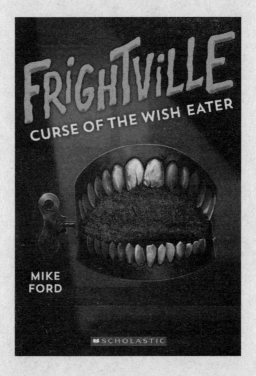

"Did you find something?" Max asked his mother for the fifth time in as many minutes.

For the fifth time she answered, "Not yet, sweetie."

They had been inside the Gingerbread House for what felt like hours. Max's mother was looking for a gift for his aunt Maxine's birthday. They were having a party for her at their house that night, and they'd already been to the grocery store for food, the florist for flowers, the party store for balloons, and the bakery for a cake. The present was the last thing on the list.

"How about this?" Max asked, picking something at random from a shelf and holding it out.

His mother looked. "I don't think Aunt Maxine would like a ceramic clown."

Max groaned and put the clown back.

"Why don't you go look around?" his mother suggested. "I won't be much longer."

"There's nothing interesting to look at," Max complained, indicating the shelves filled with candles, teacups, and bubble bath. Nothing a ten-year-old boy would want.

"Why don't you go to that new store that opened next door, then?" his mother said. "There might be something fun there. I'll be done here in a few minutes and will come meet you, okay?"

"Okay," Max said unenthusiastically. *It will probably be more boring old lady stuff*, he thought as he walked out of the Gingerbread House.

He peered into the window of the shop next door. The name was painted in red and black letters across the glass: Frightville. *Looks like a lot of old junk*, Max thought as he pushed the door open and went inside.

He was wrong. Frightville wasn't filled with junk. Max stood just inside the doorway, marveling at a room overflowing with stuff that most definitely wasn't for old ladies. At least not old ladies like his aunt Maxine.

"You look like a young man who enjoys interesting things," said a voice.

Behind the counter of the shop, a man was standing and regarding Max with an appraising air. Tall and thin, he was wearing a black suit that looked like it was probably a hundred years old. The man himself also looked like he might be a hundred years old, with pale skin and silver hair.

"This is a lot better than teacups," Max remarked.

"Oh, I have some extremely fascinating teacups," the man said, coming out from behind the counter. "They tell your fortune. But I have a feeling you're looking for something *really* special."

Max grinned. "What have you got?" he asked.

The man waved his hands around. "See for yourself," he said. "Adventure waits around every corner." He paused, raising one eyebrow.

"For those who aren't afraid to look for it," he concluded.

Max wandered around the store — checking out everything. The man was right, there *were* teacups. But there were so many other things. There was a doll that was sewn out of scraps of different patterned fabrics, a jar filled with antique keys that looked like they might unlock treasure chests, and lots of boxes with peculiar symbols on their sides that made Max wonder what might be inside them. But then he saw something *really* weird. Tucked into the dusty corner of a cupboard was a set of teeth. Max picked the teeth up and tapped his fingernail against them. He'd thought they might be wood or plastic, but they actually felt like real teeth. Or maybe they were ivory or bone. Whatever they were made of, they were old and stained, and there was a small metal key sticking out of one side. Max picked the teeth up and discovered that there was a paper tag tied to the key. Written on the tag was a short poem of sorts.

The Wish Eater

Make a wish and write it down
Place it in the Eater's mouth
Go away, come back and check
If it's gone, the answer's YES

Max turned the key attached to the teeth. The mouth swung open and a red wooden tongue emerged. He peered inside. How could a toy eat a piece of paper? It was a silly idea. But the Wish Eater *was* really cool. He'd never seen anything like it.

"Did you find something?"

Max turned and saw his mother. He held up the Wish Eater. "This," he said.

His mother made a face. "It's kind of ugly," she said. "But you've been really patient, so if you want it, it can be your reward for helping me run all these errands."

The two of them went to the counter, where Max set the Wish Eater down.

"An excellent choice," the man said as he wrapped the Wish Eater in tissue paper and placed it inside a bag. He handed the bag to Max. "May all your wishes come true."

KEY HUNTERS

UNLOCK THE ADVENTURE... ONE KEY AT A TIME!